Snobbles the Great

a SNOOZE PATCH STORY

Published by Grabkin Creatives LLC
361 Hospital Rd., Suite 521
Newport Beach, CA 92663

Distributed by Emerald Book Company

For ordering information or special discounts for bulk purchases, please contact Emerald Book Company at 4005-B Banister Lane, Three Park Place, Austin, TX 78704, (512) 891-6100.

Publisher's Cataloging-In-Publication Data
(Prepared by The Donohue Group, Inc.)

Gragg, Erika.
  Snobbles the Great : a Snooze Patch story / by Erika Gragg & Jason Dobkin. --
1st ed.

     p. : ill. ; cm.

   Summary: A snake named Snobbles must make a journey to collect fruit for his fellow snakes to eat. He only eats fruit that gives him magical powers so that he can scare off the mongoose guarding the "Forbidden Oasis" that contains all of the fruit.
   ISBN-13: 978-0-9822036-0-6
   ISBN-10: 0-9822036-0-8

1. Snakes--Juvenile fiction. 2. Magic--Juvenile fiction.   3. Adventure and adventurers--Juvenile fiction. 4. Snakes--Fiction. 5. Magic--Fiction. 6. Adventure and adventurers--Fiction. 7. Stories in rhyme. 8. Adventure stories.
I. Dobkin, Jason. II. Title.

PZ7.W734 Sn 2009   2008940109
[Fic]

Printed in Mexico

11 10 09 08   10 9 8 7 6 5 4 3 2 1

First Edition

We dedicate this tongue-twisting tale to Ryan.

Snobbles

the

Great

a SNOOZE PATCH STORY

BY

ERIKA CRAGG & JASON DOBKIN

CRABHUT CREATIVES

Sneaking and sliding around in their sleep,
Dreaming of sweet little morsels to eat,
Sensing the sun rise over them brightly,
Six snakes in the Snooze Patch slithered slightly.

Snowbra the Sultan slid in by surprise.
"Wake up, you snakes, and open your eyes!
We'll feast on fresh meats from a mongoose's den.
You'll never worry about eating again."

The snakes cheered, "Snowbra! Snip! Snip! Snooray!"
Except Snobbles, who stared at the sand in dismay.
Snobbles, the snake, didn't like eating meat.
The others all laughed, "You're missing a treat!"

Snobbles, you see, thought rodents were cute.
 He never got stuck in a wombat dispute.
In fact, he only liked swallowing fruit
And playing with his best friend, the scorpion, Scoot.

While Snobbles and Scoot talked into the night,
The other snakes drooled at the big meaty sight.
They slurped owl stew and gobbled pigeon pie,
While millions of stars shone high in the sky.

Snobbles just had to protect his friend Scoot.
　He sprung into the air to attack the big brute.
　But the mongoose jumped higher and struck Snobbles down,
　While Scoot screeched in terror, clutching the ground.

They crossed a blue river and the chase ended there.
Snobbles and Scoot shook with despair.
The mongoose loomed, his deep voice boomed.
"Me-he-he-he, have you run out of room?"

The mongoose chased after them faster and faster.
Dune turned to marsh, the air rang with laughter.
The mongoose cackled with weasely glee,
"Me catch you and eat you, you can't escape me."

he friends ran ahead, but instead of lush fruits,
They were shocked to find the evil mongoose.
He greeted them with the foulest of laughs,
"These are not trees! Just arts and crafts!"

The mongoose then snarled with a big toothy grin,
"You snakes stole me meat, now me will begin
To teach you a lesson you'll never forget.
If you steal me food, me eat you, you bet."

Snobbles had power the beast didn't know!
Eating fruits magically makes green snakes grow!
That beast jumped backward with fear in his eyes.
With magic, Snobbles grew three times in size!

he mongoose ran off in a terrible fright,
Then Snobbles and Scoot beheld a great sight.
The Forbidden Oasis so luscious and green!
Snobbles followed Scoot, who scat up the stream.

Snobbles splashed around and swam on his back.
Scoot finally asked, "Isn't it time for a snack?"
"Not yet," his friend cried, "Let's have some more fun.
Soon I'll be snacking for everyone."

To carry the fruit back to the Snooze Patch,
Snobbles opened his mouth and said, "Down the hatch."
He gulped down the fruit and lay back with a smile,
"The fruit in my belly will last us a while."

Back in the Snooze Patch, the snakes were amazed
When Snobbles and Scoot slunk out from the haze.
"I Shmee Shmobbles!" shmumbled Snack Mamba.
And they all started slithering the silly snake samba!

Snobbles belched up a BIG belly of fruit.

The snakes of the Snooze Patch cheered, "Snobbles! Yahoo!"

Snowbra relaxed, Snocrates barbecued,

Scoot got fruit for Snoo-Billy Doo.

Snack Mamba and Snoliver were stuck like glue,

Snattle-Tale looked for gossip to stew, and

Snobbles played snake-ball with Snaggletooth too.

And the snakes all considered, but none could conclude

Where the sneck Snobbles fit all that food.